For Mia, my little bean
—R. K. D.

For Julie T.
—A. L.

Atheneum Books for Young Readers
An imprint of Simon & Schuster Children's Publishing Division
1230 Avenue of the Americas
New York, New York 10020
Text copyright © 2009 by Rebecca Kai Dotlich
Illustrations copyright © 2009 by Aileen Leijten
All rights reserved, including the right of reproduction in whole or in part in any form.
Book design by Sonia Chaghatzbanian
The text for this book is set in Odette.
Illustrations were rendered in graphite pencil and painted in Photoshop.
Manufactured in China
First Edition
2 4 6 8 10 9 7 5 3 1
Library of Congress Cataloging-in-Publication Data
Dotlich, Rebecca Kai.
Bella & Bean / Rebecca Kai Dotlich ; illustrated by Aileen Leijten.—1st ed.
p. cm.
Summary: When Bean constantly distracts her while she tries to write, Bella finds her poems taking unexpected
and silly twists, till she realizes she has written a wonderful poem about her best friend.
ISBN-13: 978-0-689-85616-7
ISBN-10: 0-689-85616-4
[1. Poetry—Fiction. 2. Best friends—Fiction. 3. Friendship—Fiction.]
I. Leijten, Aileen, ill. II. Title. III. Title: Bella and Bean.
PZ7.D73735Be 2009
[E]—dc22   2007034447

Bella & Bean

story by

Rebecca Kai Dotlich

illustrations by

Aileen Leijten

Atheneum Books for Young Readers
New York   London   Toronto   Sydney

lexile 520

Bella lived in an old brick house with white shutters, just up the hill from Spoon Pond.

Every day she wrote poetry at a small desk, beneath a small window, shaded by a canopy the color of plums.

One spring morning her best friend, Bean, poked her head in the window.

"Yoo-hoo, Bella,"

said Bean. "See my new hat?"

"I don't have time for hats, Bean," said Bella. "I'm writing new poems."

Bean jiggled her head. "Aren't these daisies just divine?" she asked.

"I can't think about rivers and moons when you are talking about hats," said Bella.

"Why do you *have* to think about rivers and moons?" asked Bean.

"Poets just do," said Bella.

"Well," said Bean, "maybe you should think about rivers and moons *and* hats."

"Maybe," said Bella, "I should think about closing my window."

"My," said Bean, "aren't we grumpy."

Bella watched as Bean walked down to Spoon Pond, hat flopping in the breeze, yellow-eyed daisies bobbing like small suns.

A walk to the pond would be lovely, thought Bella. But she really just wanted to finish her poems.

And so she did.

She wrote words that reminded her of the river: bend, flow, gurgle, and rush.

She wrote words that reminded her of the moon: white, round, silver, and bright.

She wiggled just right in her chair and added: flower, bonnet, sun, and breeze.

Then Bella wrote this poem:

The river gurgles 'round the bend.
It rushes like the breeze.
The sun is a silver bonnet.
The stones are its flowers.

Bella was deep in thought when Bean tapped on the window ledge.

Bella looked out to see one Bean leg, kicked high in the air.

"Like my foot?" asked Bean.

"I don't have time for feet," said Bella.

Bean pushed a daisy out of her eye. "Well, do you like it?"

Bella sighed. "Feet are *feet*."

"Look," said Bean. "My toes go in order from big to small, and not one of them lops over the other."

Bella rolled her eyes as she wrote.

"I've been told I have the cutest toes," said Bean, turning her foot this way and that.

"Who told you that?" asked Bella.

"Secret," said Bean. And she swung her leg back down to the ground.

"Well, here's a secret for you," said Bella. "Poets need peace and quiet."

"Peace and quiet with a pinch of grump," muttered Bean.

Bella tapped her pen to her chin.
She wrote:

Bonnets, daisies, windows, toes—
Secrets hide in sky, in rose.

And then something big and green caught Bella's eye.

"Bean, is that you under there?"

Bean popped up.
"It's me, it's me!"
she cried.

Bella crossed her arms and peered out the window. *"What is it?"*

"Well," said Bean. "Looks like *somebody* needs a nap."

Bella tapped her fingers on the window ledge. "I'm waiting. . . ."

Bean talked fast. "I'm going to Spoon Pond to plant my most beautiful snow bush, and I'm inviting you."

Bella shook her head. "I don't have time for planting when I'm writing poetry."

"Phooey!" said Bean. "Can't you write poetry *and* plant?"

"Absolutely not," said Bella. "I'm thinking of words."

Bean scrunched her nose. "Maybe you should think about the word 'Bean,'" she said.

"Maybe *you* should think about the word 'good-bye,'" said Bella, and she shut her window.

Bella watched Bean drag
the snow bush behind her
like a summer sleigh.

Then she finished her poem:

Beautiful snow bush,
Loveliest I've seen,
This is my wish:
Bloom wild for Bean.

And she stuck it on the bulletin board
next to Bean's picture.

Bella
wrote
all
morning.

She wrote through lunch.

She wrote between bites
of her supper sandwich.

When the clock chimed eight,
Bella looked out her window.

The sun was gone.
The sky poured stars
like sugar.

Bella loved stars.

"Star," she said aloud. *"Star,"* she whispered as she wrote it on her paper. And she began . . .

My friend is a star, she wrote. She thought of more words. And more again.

She thought about Bean showing off her feet, and she laughed.

She does have the cutest toes.

Bella dialed Bean's number.

Bean let her phone ring three times. "Hello, Ruby Bean on the line," she said.

"Want to meet at the pond?" asked Bella.

Bean popped a strawberry into her mouth. "I thought," she said, "you were busy thinking of words."

"I was," said Bella. "And I thought of the word 'Bean.'"

Bean grabbed her hat. "I'm on my way, and I'm not lion," she giggled.

Bean arrived at the pond holding a blanket, a pencil, a notebook, and something behind her back.

"What's behind your back?" asked Bella.

"Surprise!" yelled Bean.

"Why, it's *just* like yours," said Bella as she placed the hat on her head.

Bean clapped. "Now we *both* look divine." She closed her eyes. "I'm ready for poems."

Bella stretched out on the blanket, and one by one, read her poems to Bean under the starry sky.

Besides **river** and **moon** and **daisy**, Bean heard words like **bonnet** and **bush** and **breeze**.

"Your poems make me melt," said Bean.
"Don't you dare," said Bella.

Bean began pedaling in the air. "Some of them rhyme and some of them don't," she said. "I got that right away."

Bella reached into her pocket and
pulled out a neatly folded piece
of paper. "One poem to go,"
she said.

"Goody," said Bean.
She closed her eyes tight
as she pedaled.

Bella read:

My friend is a star,
My friend is a rose,
My best friend Bean
Has the cutest toes.

"*I'm a poem!*"
shouted Bean.

"I'm famous."

"For cute toes."
Bella giggled.

Bean popped up.
"Let's write a poem about us!"
She opened her small notebook and wrote three words:
Friend. Cozy. And sky. She held her notebook high in the air.
"Ta-da."

This time, *Bella* clapped.

"It came to me," said Bean, snapping her fingers, *"just like that!"*

"Your turn," said Bean. So Bella added three new words. **Blanket.** **Pond.** And **moon.**

"Goody!" said Bean. She kicked off her sandals and flopped on her back.

Bella kept writing.

Bean rolled from one side of the blanket to the other, and back again.

She looked up. Bella was still writing. "You are poem *crazy*," said Bean as she rolled again from side to side.

Bella kept writing.

"I'm dizzy,"
said Bean.

"No wonder,"
said Bella.

Bean sat up. Bella was *still* writing.
"Is our poem done yet?" asked Bean.
Bella tapped the pencil to her chin.
"I need just one more word."

Bean sighed. "You take forever."

Calm

"That's it!"
cried Bella.

ON

One blanket
holds two friends
calm and cozy
at the edge of a pond.
The moon looks like
a clock in the sky
with the big hand on
Forever.

The end

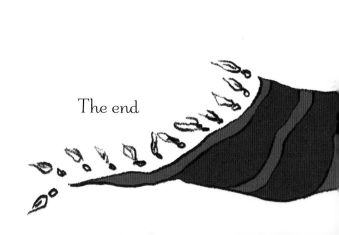